# Some words about Sports Day:

"Good cluck!!!"
*A friendly chicken*

"Sniff my sweat!"
*Jack Beechwhistle*

"Look at my kitchen floor!"
*Daisy's mum*

"Puff, pant, gasp, oops!"
*Daisy*

"You'll you'll never never
beat beat us us!!"
*Lottie and Dottie*

**"Run, Daisy, run!"**
*Gabby's teddy*

# More Daisy adventures!

DAISY AND THE TROUBLE WITH NATURE

DAISY AND THE TROUBLE WITH LIFE

DAISY AND THE TROUBLE WITH ZOOS

DAISY AND THE TROUBLE WITH GIANTS

DAISY AND THE TROUBLE WITH KITTENS

DAISY AND THE TROUBLE WITH CHRISTMAS

DAISY AND THE TROUBLE WITH MAGGOTS

DAISY AND THE TROUBLE WITH COCONUTS

DAISY AND THE TROUBLE WITH BURGLARS

DAISY AND THE TROUBLE WITH PIGGY BANKS

DAISY AND THE TROUBLE WITH VAMPIRES

DAISY AND THE TROUBLE WITH CHOCOLATE

DAISY AND THE TROUBLE WITH SCHOOL TRIPS

DAISY AND THE TROUBLE WITH NATURE

JACK BEECHWHISTLE: ATTACK OF THE GIANT SLUGS

JACK BEECHWHISTLE: RISE OF THE HAIRY HORROR

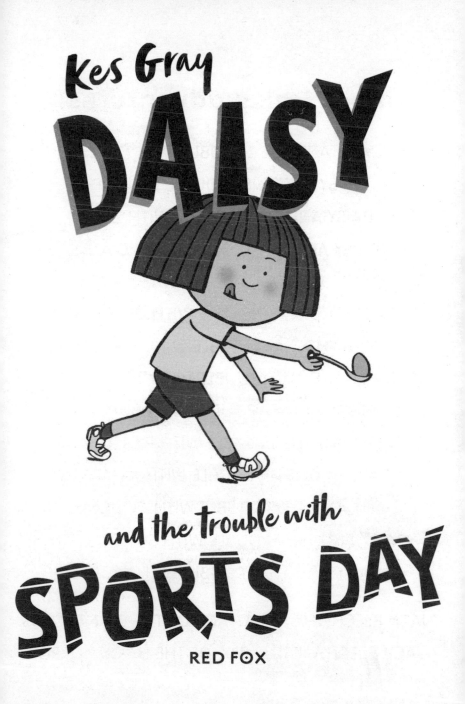

Kes Gray

# DAISY

and the trouble with

# SPORTS DAY

RED FOX

RED FOX

UK | USA | Canada | Ireland | Australia
India | New Zealand | South Africa

Red Fox is part of the Penguin Random House group of companies
whose addresses can be found at global.penguinrandomhouse.com.

www.penguin.co.uk
www.puffin.co.uk
www.ladybird.co.uk

Penguin
Random House
UK

First published 2017
This edition published 2020

001

Set in VAG Rounded Light 15pt/23pt
Printed in Great Britain by Clays Ltd, Elcograf S.p.A.

A CIP catalogue record for this book is available from the British Library

ISBN: 978–1–782–95970–0

All correspondence to
Red Fox, Penguin Random House Children's
One Embassy Gardens,
8 Viaduct Gardens, London SW11 7BW

MIX
Paper from
responsible sources
FSC® C018179

Penguin Random House is committed to a
sustainable future for our business, our readers
and our planet. This book is made from Forest
Stewardship Council® certified paper.

# To the Bradys

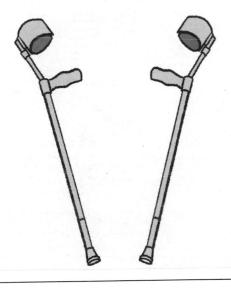

# CHAPTER 1

The **trouble with Sports Day** is everyone in my school wants to win. If children didn't want to win so much then I would never have had to go into Olympic training.

Winning a race on Sports Day can be really difficult, especially if there are other people in the race. Double especially if the other people in the race are really fast runners. Triply especially if your mum won't buy you a new pair of trainers, and fourply especially if she won't even buy you a new headband.

Athletes on the telly say that if you want to come first in a race then you have to get "into the zone". The only zone I ended up in after Sports Day was the headmaster's office.

Which isn't my fault!

# CHAPTER 2

It was nearly two weeks ago when our Sports Day was announced. We were in Monday morning assembly and the whole school had just got told off by Mr Copford for being too chatty and fidgety. Mr Copford is our new headmaster. He's really cool (unless you're being told off), but he looked even cooler that morning, because instead of wearing a grey suit like he normally does, he was wearing a red tracksuit and white trainers! Plus he had a whistle around his neck!!

The **trouble with whistles** is as soon as you see one hanging around a headmaster's neck it makes you want to chat and fidget. Especially if the whistle is a sports whistle.

I think to start off with Mr Copford was going to save his special Sports Day announcement until after he had given us our Thought for the Week, but when our chatting and fidgeting got out of control, he decided to do the Sports Day announcement first.

Second, actually. First he had to blow his whistle really loudly.

The **trouble with blowing sports whistles really loudly** is it makes you jump. Especially if you're in an assembly hall that echoes.

As soon as the assembly hall went quiet, Mr Copford went straight on with his special Sports Day announcement. He said our Sports Day would be happening in just over a week's time and that our parents were allowed to come and watch us do our races!

Then things got even more exciting. Because instead of making us sing a song about Jesus, Mr Copford held up the Sports Day cup! The Sports Day cup is given to the house that wins the most points at the end of all the races!

There are four houses in our school. All of them are named after types of pasta. I'm in Tagliatelle and Gabby is in Fettuccine. The ones we're not in are Penne and Linguine.

The **trouble with pastas** is that when you see them written down you don't know how to say them. Because they are in Italian.

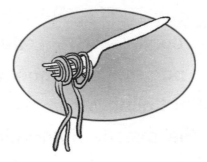

The proper Italian way to say tagliatelle is "tally a telly" (except everyone in my school says "taggly a telly" instead).

The proper Italian way to say fettuccine is "fettoo cheeny" (except most people in my school have changed it a little bit to "fetter cheeny").

If you're Italian and you're saying penne you're meant to say "pennay" (some people in my school say "penny" but me and Gabby say it the proper Italian way).

And the exactly right Italian way to say linguine is "lin gweeny" (which is the way absolutely everyone in my school says it, even Jack Beechwhistle).

If you ask me, having Italian-sounding house names is a really good idea, because it means if you ever go abroad you are able to speak the language. Especially if you go to a restaurant and you want pasta.

After Mr Copford had done his Sports Day announcement, he gave us our Thought for the Week.

Our Thought for the Week was, "Silence is golden. So let's go for gold."

The **trouble with Thoughts for the Week** is sometimes they can be a bit confusing.

I mean, I never knew silence was golden. In fact, I never knew silence was the colour of anything at all. Because it's a sound and not an actual thing.

Except it isn't. Because silence *can't* be a sound, because it's the sound of no sound. Which means it's the sound of nothing. Which is nothing. So it must be the colour of nothing. Which is nothing.

When we got back to our classroom, I asked Gabby what colour she thought silence was. She said she didn't know. But when she closed her eyes and listened to the silence really carefully, it looked black.

Not golden.

So I closed my eyes and listened really hard. And she was right. Except when I scrunched my eyes up really tight, the silence I was listening to stopped being the colour of black and started being the colour of black with little white dots.

Not golden.

So we asked some of our friends what colour they thought silence was.

Sanjay Lapore said he thought silence was purple with green stripes. Melanie Simpson said she thought silence was sky blue pink, and Vicky Carrow said she thought silence was the colour of whale custard.

That's **the trouble with Vicky Carrow**. She's always saying things that are silly.

In the end, everyone decided to ignore the first half of Mr Copford's Thought for the Week and just concentrate on the second half instead. After all, everybody knows what "go for gold" means. It means do everything you can to win. WIN, WIN, WIN!

# CHAPTER 3

It was Wednesday before Mrs Peters told us which Sports Day races we would be in.

She didn't tell us straight away. First of all we had to do Sports Day rehearsals.

The **trouble with Sports Day rehearsals** is it was a bit hot.

Plus I put my PE shirt on inside-out without knowing. Which was really annoying, because no one told me when we ran out onto the field.

It was really, really sunny on the field, even though it was still only the morning. Gabby said she really hoped she would be chosen to do the sixty-metre sprint.

Which was really strange, because so did I!

Then she said she would like to do the multi-skills race as well.

Which was even stranger, because I wanted to do the multi-skills race as well as well!

In case you've never been in a Sports Day, sixty-metre sprints are when you have to run as fast as you can for sixty metres and be the first one to get to the end.

Multi-skills is when you have to throw a bean bag into a hoop, dribble a football, bounce a tennis ball on a tennis racquet, put on a hat and a shirt and then take them off, balance a bean bag on your head and be the first one to get to the end.

You have to be a really good athlete to do multi-skills.

After Mrs Peters had clapped her hands loudly a few times, we all sat in a circle on the grass. Mrs Peters told us there would be ten different Sports Day events to choose from and that if we especially wanted to

be in one, we should raise our hand high above our head when she read it out.

I was so excited I put my hand up straight away. But then I took it down really quickly. Because do you know what Mrs Peters said next? I couldn't believe it. And neither could Gabby.

Just as me and Gabby were totally about to get into the zone, Mrs Peters took a pen and a piece of paper out of her tracksuit top pocket and said that everyone in the class would be able to compete in one event only!

ONE EVENT ONLY!

Starting with . . .

. . . the sack race.

The **trouble with sack races** is it's really hard to run fast when your legs are in a sack. Plus it's really easy to fall over.

So no one put their hand up.

So Mrs Peters said, "Foam javelin."

The **trouble with foam javelins** is they're made of foam.

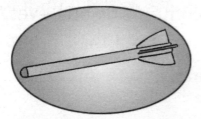

Which isn't a proper metal. Which means they're not like proper spears.

So no one put their hand up.

So Mrs Peters said, "Shot putt."

The **trouble with shot putts** is the ones in our PE cupboard are made of foam too.

Plus they don't even go as far as a foam javelin or a foam discus. Not even with the wind behind you.

So no one put their hand up.

So Mrs Peters said, "Sixty-metre sprint."

The **trouble with saying sixty-metre sprint** is I was still thinking about foam when Mrs Peters said it. By the time I put my hand up, everyone had their hand up.

Mrs Peters said it wouldn't be possible for everyone in the class to do the sixty-metre sprint, especially as there were two other classes in our year that would be racing with us too.

So she said, "Multi-skills" instead.

The moment Mrs Peters said, "Multi-skills" I put my hand straight up into the air as fast as a rocket and waved it as high as I could. Trouble is, so did everyone else.

So I tried to get my hand even higher.

But so did everyone else.

So I tried to lift my bottom up off the grass while I was still cross-legged.

But so did everyone else.

The **trouble with lifting your bottom up off the grass while you're cross-legged** is it makes you lose your balance.

Especially if you're waving one hand really high in the air at the same time.

So I fell over.

And so did everyone else.

# CHAPTER 4

It took Mrs Peters about five minutes to get everyone untangled and back into a circle.

I think we could have untangled faster, but some people were definitely tangling on purpose, especially Jack Beechwhistle and Harry Bayliss.

Once Mrs Peters had told Jack and Harry off for tangling on purpose and made them sit on opposite sides of the circle, she said that if we couldn't volunteer for Sports Day events without all putting our hands up at the same time, then she would have to choose our events for us, starting with Harry and Jack who would be serving cream teas to parents if they weren't careful.

The **trouble with serving cream teas to parents** is it isn't a proper Sports Day thing at all.

You don't get to run or throw anything at all. I don't think you even get a sticker.

Harry and Jack were really well-behaved after that. Even during our warm-up.

The **trouble with warm-ups** is you have to do them before you can get to do proper racing. Even if the sun is really hot and you're warm enough already.

Mrs Peters told us that warm-ups

are the most important part of any athlete's race preparations, because they loosen up your muscles and get your heart pumping. I didn't really want to do warm-ups at all. I just wanted to go straight onto the racing bit, but we didn't have any choice.

First of all we had to do stretching.

The **trouble with stretching** is it really stretches you, especially if you do really stretchy stretches. My stretches were far more stretchy than Mrs Peters'.

In fact, no one did stretches as stretchy as me. Which meant by the time I'd done my stretchiest stretch, my legs were really aching. Especially the backs of my knees.

After we'd done stretching, we had to do running on the spot.

The **trouble with running on the spot** is you don't go anywhere. So you can't tell how fast you're going.

I must have gone really, really fast because by the time I'd stopped running I was really, really out of puff.

Gabby said if I had paced myself during the warm-up, I would still have had some energy left for the actual rehearsals. But I said if we wanted to get picked for our favourite races we had to get straight into the zone.

The first race we rehearsed was the hurdles.

The **trouble with hurdles** is the hurdles get in the way when you're running. Which is why I came fifth.

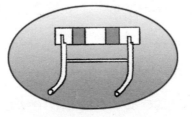

The second race we rehearsed was the space hoppers.

The **trouble with space hoppers** is sometimes they bounce sideways instead of forward. Which is why I came sixth.

The third race we rehearsed was the obstacle race.

The **trouble with obstacle races** is there are loads of obstacles in the way.

Which is why I came last.

I was actually quite pleased when we rehearsed the foam javelin, because it gave me a chance to get my breath back. Trouble is, every time I let go of my javelin the sun got in my eyes, plus I think the wind might have been blowing the wrong way, too. Anyway, I didn't do very well in that either.

Or the foam discus.

When I went back to the running track to get ready for the sixty-metre sprint, the ache in the back of my knees had gone all the way up to my arms.

That's the **trouble with throwing things made of foam**. It makes your shoulders come out of their arm-holes.

There were eight girls in my sixty-metre sprint rehearsal. I was in lane three, Fiona Tucker was in lane one, Stephanie Brakespeare was in lane two, Jasmine Smart was in lane four, Nishta Baghwat was in lane five, Paula Potts was in lane six, Liberty Pearce was in lane seven and Vicky Carrow was meant to be in lane eight but she was being silly again.

I was easily the fastest girl out of all of us, so I was sure I was going to win. Trouble is, just before Mrs Peters said, "Go" I realized my shirt was inside-out. Which made me get out of the zone.

The **trouble with being out of the zone** is it makes your legs stop running as fast as they can run. And it makes your shoelaces come undone.

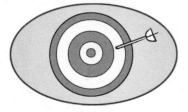

Which is why I came seventh.

I beat Vicky Carrow by about forty

metres, but I'm not sure she really understands what "sprint" means.

Gabby said she reckoned I'd definitely done too much stretching and running on the spot during our warm-ups, and she was sure I'd do better in the multi-skills.

Trouble is, we never got a chance to find out. Because we ran out of time. Which was really annoying, because I'd just done my shoelaces up into a double knot!

Mrs Peters said she was very sorry we had to stop, but we only had an hour to practise in and it was time to go in for lunch. Then she said that if we had all sat in a circle nicely in the first place instead of rolling around on the grass and tangling on purpose, we might have had time to do the multi-skills race as well as all the other events we hadn't had time to do.

Which was totally Jack Beech-whistle's and Harry Bayliss's fault!

# CHAPTER 5

The **trouble with lunch time** is it gave Mrs Peters time to forget how deliberately tangled Jack and Harry had been.

Which meant when she read out the Sports Day events that we would all be doing, she didn't make Jack and Harry serve cream teas to parents at all. She said they could

both do the sixty-metre sprint!

If I was a teacher and two children in my class had got deliberately tangled on the grass, I would have made them serve cream teas AND do the washing-up afterwards. And wear pink rubber gloves and a frilly apron each.

Gabby totally agreed with me, but she wouldn't stop smiling because Mrs Peters had chosen her for the girls' sixty-metre sprint too.

At first, I felt a little bit jealous, because I knew that with my shoelaces double knotted and my PE shirt outside-in, I could definitely go for gold in the sixty-metre sprint. But then I reckoned that if I wasn't in the sixty-metre sprint, I was bound to be in the multi-skills race.

But I wasn't.

I wasn't doing the long-distance running race either.

I wasn't doing the sack race.

I wasn't doing the obstacle race.

I wasn't doing the space hoppers.

Or the hurdles.

Or the foam javelin.

Or the foam shot putt.

Or the foam anything.

The race Mrs Peters had written me down for was a race called the egg and spoon.

The **trouble with the egg and spoon** is it's a race with an egg and a spoon.

Which makes it really difficult to race. Because eggs and spoons can't go very fast.

Because they are so wobbly.

At first when Mrs Peters said, "Egg and spoon" I went a bit hot.

Then when Jack Beechwhistle started laughing and pointing at me I went a bit red.

Gabby said to take no notice of Jack Beechwhistle and that the egg and spoon race was one of the best races to be in, as long as your egg doesn't fall off your spoon.

Which made me get a bit worried.

When I found out that Lottie and Dottie Taylor had been chosen to do the egg and spoon too, I got even more worried.

Lottie and Dottie Taylor are identical twins. They go to proper running club at the weekends AND after school! Plus they are so fast and so identical they always come joint-first in their races with the same identical times!

Gabby said it didn't matter how fast Lottie and Dottie were, because egg and spoon races weren't just about being fast, they were more about keeping your egg on your spoon. She said that if I did lots of egg and spoon practising before Sports Day, she was sure I would be able to beat Lottie and Dottie, especially if I got into the zone.

Which made me feel a bit better.

Then Gabby said we could share zones after school by practising our races in our back gardens.

Which made me feel a lot better.

But then Jack Beechwhistle started laughing and pointing at me again.

Which made me feel a lot worse.

By the time I left school on Wednesday, I didn't know whether I wanted to be in the egg and spoon race or not.

I didn't even know if I wanted to be in Sports Day at all!

# CHAPTER 6

When Gabby and I started our first training session after school on Thursday, I started to feel much better.

Until I broke my first egg.

Gabby and me had only been in the zone for about twenty seconds when my first egg got broken on the kitchen floor.

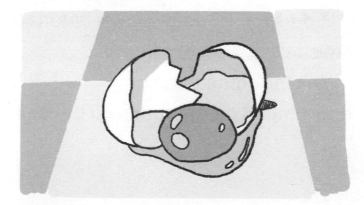

I didn't drop it. It fell out of the spoon all by itself.

Luckily, Mum was in the front garden watering the flowers, so she didn't hear it crack. Or see the mess. Even luckier, there was a box of twelve eggs in the fridge that we could keep training with. Well, eleven.

After my first egg broke, Gabby said it might be better if I learned to walk with an egg and spoon before I tried to run with an egg and spoon.

So I took it really slowly the next time.

But the same thing happened. The egg jumped off my spoon all by itself.

The **trouble with two eggs breaking on the kitchen floor** is it makes twice as much mess. Trouble is, I was still trying to get the hang of keeping an egg on my spoon. So I didn't have time to clear it up.

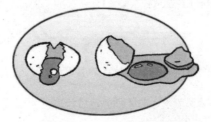

Gabby said it might be better if I tried a bigger spoon, so I changed from a teaspoon to a pudding spoon.

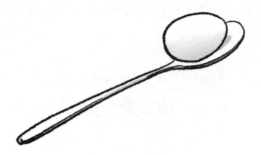

But that didn't work either.

So I changed from a pudding spoon to a cooking spoon.

The **trouble with cooking spoons** is they give eggs too much space to roll about in.

The **trouble with rolling-about eggs** is it's absolutely impossible to keep them on the spoon.

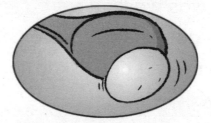

So I dropped the next egg as well.

Gabby said that when I got my next egg, it might be a good idea if I tried to hold my spoon with two hands instead of one. That way, I would be able to keep my egg a bit more steady when I was walking.

So I got another spoon from the kitchen drawer and asked her to show me how.

But her egg fell off and broke too.

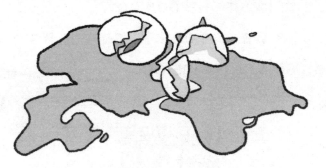

So we both had to try again.
But both of those eggs fell off and broke too.

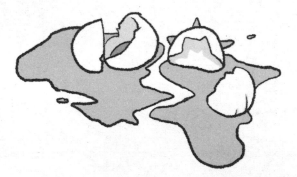

Which meant we only had four eggs left in the box now.

So we decided to do our training on soft grass instead.

When we got outside onto my lawn, we did a little bit of stretching

and a tiny bit of running on the spot first, and then we really concentrated on getting into the zone-zone.

Zone-zones are the next one up from zones. If you're in the zone-zone you REALLY, REALLY are going for gold!

Gabby said that if I wanted to beat Lottie and Dottie Taylor, then practising in my back garden was a much better idea, because it would give me a longer space to walk around with my egg and spoon. Plus grass is a lot softer than kitchen floors. Especially if your mum has been too lazy to cut it.

The first time I dropped my ninth egg it didn't even break!

It did break the second time, but by then I had got to the clothesline!

I didn't break my tenth egg until I'd got all the way to my shed! Plus, when I broke it, I wasn't just walking – I was almost nearly running!

Once I had started almost nearly running with my egg and spoon,

Gabby said she would start timing me by counting how long it took me to get to the wall at the end of my garden and back.

Which made me a bit wobbly the first time, because I'd never been timed by someone before. Which is why my eleventh egg didn't count.

Once I started almost nearly running with my twelfth egg, though, I didn't just get into the zone-zone, I got into the zone-zone-zone!!! In fact, I got all the way to the garden wall and back in twenty-three and a bit counts! Plus I only dropped my egg twice along the way.

Gabby told me that I had done my first ever PB!

PB means "Personal Best". Which means my Personal Best egg and spoon racing time was twenty-three and a bit!

Trouble is, just as I set off to get my second PB, my mum screamed my twelfth egg out of my spoon.

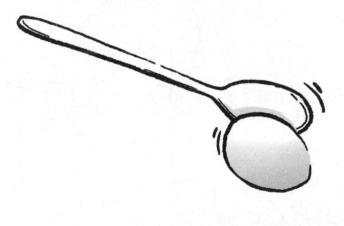

It wasn't just my mum's scream that made my egg jump out of my spoon and break, it was the sound of the watering can clanging too.

When me and Gabby looked round, we saw my mum sitting on the floor in the kitchen.

At first I thought she might have been a bit tired after watering the flowers, but then I realized she had slipped over on some broken eggs.

About eight broken eggs, actually.

The **trouble with eight broken eggs** is they are really skiddy, especially if you tread on them when you're not looking.

Double especially if you're holding a watering can.

When my mum asked me what on earth I thought I had been doing with her eggs, I told her that me and Gabby had been going for gold.

Trouble is, my mum had more yellow on her than gold.

"YOU'RE SUPPOSED TO BOIL THEM FIRST!" she said – well, shouted.

"IF YOU BOIL THE EGGS FIRST, THEY WON'T BREAK WHEN THEY FALL OFF YOUR SPOON! DO YOU KNOW HOW MUCH EGGS COST, DAISY? DO YOU THINK EGGS GROW ON TREES, DAISY??! WELL, EGGS DON'T GROW ON TREES AND NEITHER DO OMELETTES, OR PANCAKES, OR CAKE MIXES OR ANYTHING ELSE THAT YOU FIND EGGS IN!!!"

Which actually isn't true.

"Birds do," I said. "Birds grow on trees and they've got eggs inside them. There are eggs inside birds' bottoms."

Now that I think about it, I'm not

sure that talking to my mum about birds' bottoms was a very good idea. But it did give Gabby a good idea of her own: to say goodbye very quickly and do her sixty-metre sprint training on her way home.

# CHAPTER 7

The **trouble with breaking twelve eggs** is it makes your mum act really strange.

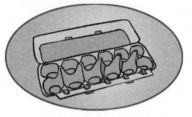

Do you know what my mum gave me for tea on Thursday evening after Gabby had gone home? Egg and bacon with *no egg*.

And then do you know what she put in my lunch box when she was making my sandwiches for school? Egg sandwiches with *no egg*. I didn't say anything, though. I pretended I hadn't noticed.

But then she forced me to notice, because she started opening and closing the fridge door and talking to herself in a really loud voice.

"I think I'll bake a cake this evening. OOOHHH, LOOK! No eggs!"

"I think I'll make some Yorkshire puddings this weekend. OOOHHH, LOOK! No eggs!"

"I think I'll rustle up some eggy-bread. OOOHHH, LOOK! No eggs!"

If you ask me, opening and closing

a fridge door on purpose over and over again is a really bad thing to do, especially when it's a really hot evening, because all of the hot air from the summer could get into the fridge and make everything inside melt and go mouldy.

Which means if my mum hadn't stopped opening and closing the fridge door on purpose, we could have ended up with no butter, no jam, no lettuce, no tomatoes, no fruit juice, no yoghurts, no ham, no jellies and no Dairylea triangles either. Which would have been much worse than just having no eggs.

It was about quarter to seven before Mum stopped talking to herself in a loud voice about no eggs.

Honestly, I've never been so pleased to get into a bath.

The **trouble with baths** is once you've filled them up with water and bubble bath, they make your writing paper go soggy. And the ink in your pen stop writing.

I had to take my pad and my pen into my bath, because I'd had a brilliant idea while I was walking up the stairs.

The **trouble with brilliant ideas** is you have to write them down straight away. Especially if they're going to help you go for gold!

The first brilliant idea I had was to write me and Gabby a proper "Go for Gold Exercise and Training Plan". Go for Gold Exercise and Training Plans are things that proper athletes use to make sure they will have enough puff to win their races. The exercises are really tough, but you know what athletes say – when the tough isn't going, then the going isn't tough.

This is the Go for Gold Exercise and Training Plan that I wrote in the bath:

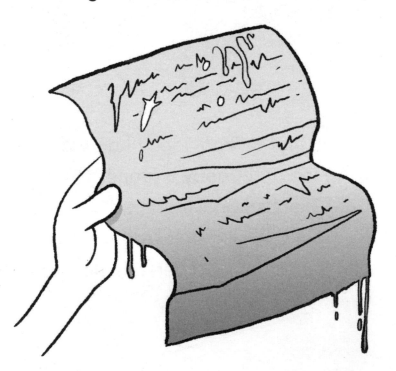

And this is the one I re-did in my bedroom:

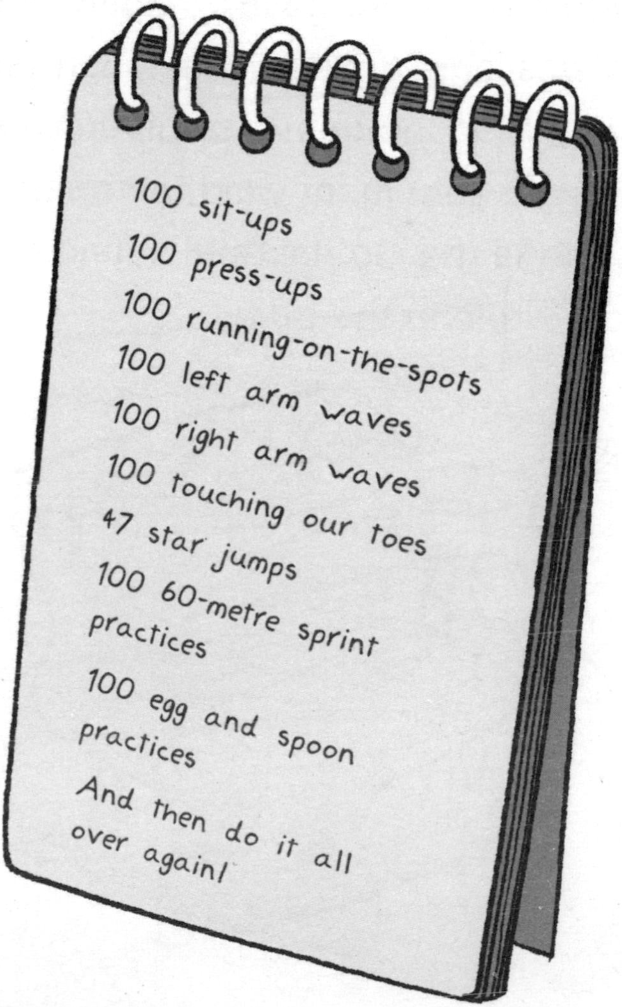

100 sit-ups
100 press-ups
100 running-on-the-spots
100 left arm waves
100 right arm waves
100 touching our toes
47 star jumps
100 60-metre sprint practices

100 egg and spoon practices

And then do it all over again!

The second brilliant idea I had was to write me and Gabby a really good "Go for Gold Eating Plan". Go for Gold Eating Plans are recipes that make sure proper athletes eat all the right things to help them win their races.

This is the Go for Gold Eating Plan that I wrote in the bath:

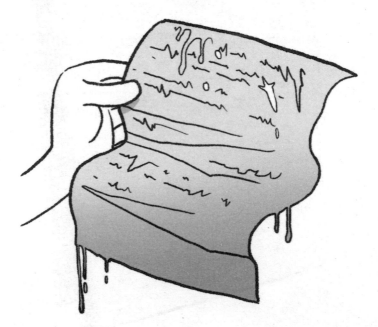

And this is the one I re-did in my
bedroom:

Lemonade
Cheese and onion crisps
Dry-roasted peanuts
Twiglets
Mars bars
Cheese strings

When I read them to Gabby over the phone, she thought they were brilliant. Except maybe we should have normal-roasted peanuts instead of dry ones.

When I told her that once my mum had forgotten about the broken eggs I would ask her to add everything to her shopping list, Gabby said it might be better to wait a while because sometimes mums can stay quite cross about having no eggs.

But by the time I had put my pyjamas on and got under my covers on Thursday, Mum seemed to have forgotten all about the broken eggs. Not only did she sit down on my bed, she helped me dry my hair and then brush it. She even said she would tell me a bedtime story!

She seemed in such a good mood that I almost nearly showed her my Go for Gold Eating Plan right there and then! But I'm glad I didn't . . .

. . . because then I found out what my bedtime story was going to be. It was going to be the story of Humpty Dumpty.

Oh no, it wasn't.

No eggs . . .

# CHAPTER 8

When Gabby and me got to school on Friday, it seemed like absolutely everyone in our class was going for gold!

Liberty Pearce had a granola bar in her lunch box, Daniel Carrington had an energy drink in his rucksack, Fiona Tucker had her hair tied extra back, Sanjay Lapore's mum had given him a vitamin C tablet three days in a row, Jasmine Smart had switched to white sports socks instead of white ankle socks.

Trouble is, Jack Beechwhistle was wearing a new pair of trainers.

The **trouble with new pairs of trainers** is you're absolutely not allowed to wear them to school.

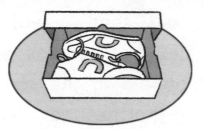

The **trouble with even old pairs of trainers** is you're not allowed to wear them to school either.

Which is really annoying because there is no way that Jack Beechwhistle should have been wearing any types of trainers to school.

But he was.

Jack said that I was totally jealous and that he was going to be unstoppable in the sixty-metre sprint now that he had a new pair of trainers to go for gold in. Then he started calling his new pair of trainers "bad boys". Which was really, really annoying. And then he called me an egg on legs. Which was REALLY, REALLY, REALLY annoying.

And untrue.

Which is why I told Mrs Peters.

The **trouble with telling Mrs Peters about Jack Beechwhistle** is it never does any good. When Jack told her that his dog had eaten his school shoes and his mum and dad wouldn't be able to buy him a new pair until the weekend, she believed him.

So he was allowed to wear his new trainers ALL DAY! Which was even more annoying, because every time I saw him in the playground, he started running really fast on the spot and then leaning back and doing a Usain Bolt point at the sky.

The **trouble with doing Usain Bolt points at the sky** is it's a really show-offy thing to do. Unless you're Usain Bolt.

Jack said he was the next Usain Bolt and that by the time he was fifteen he would probably be the fastest runner in the world. Especially now that he had a new headband to wear as well.

The **trouble with new headbands** is they are show-offy too, especially if no one else in the school is wearing one.

When Jack put his new headband on at morning break to show everyone, all the children in my class gathered round him and clapped and cheered him.

Except me.

Gabby said she thought Jack Beechwhistle looked quite funny in a headband and school uniform. But I didn't. I thought he looked like a disgrace to athletics.

At lunch time, me and Gabby sat as far away from him in the dinner hall as we possibly could, but he still did Usain Bolt points at us with his sandwiches. And his Fruit Shoot.

Then things got even worse, because when we went outside to play in the playground, not only did Jack Beechwhistle have his new headband on again, but this time he was wearing two brand-new wristbands too!

Jack said that after he had won the sixty-metre sprint on Sports Day he was going to collect all the winning sweat from his headband

and wristbands and have it made into
a new sports perfume for men called
"Beechwhistle". And if we were lucky,
he might let me and Gabby sniff it.

I said I would rather sniff the stinkiest poo in the world than go near his new perfume.

So he called me a poo-lover.

So I called him Poosain Bolt.

So he called me Egg Leg Smegg.

So I told the dinner ladies.

The good thing about telling the dinner ladies about Jack Beechwhistle is they always do something about it, because they like me more than him.

When Jack told them that he was wearing a headband and wristbands for medical reasons and that his dog had eaten his note from the doctor, they didn't believe him.

They didn't believe him so much, they took his headband and wristbands off him and told him he couldn't have them back until the end of the day!

Which served the back of his head

right, because the next time he tried to do another Usain Bolt point at me in class, he leaned too far back and fell off his chair!!!

HA!

# CHAPTER 9

When we came out of school on Friday, Gabby and me had decided to completely ignore Jack Beechwhistle. Even if he did Usain Bolt points at us.

Trouble is, as soon as we got outside the school gates, he caught us up. AND this time he was eating chewing gum!

The **trouble with eating chewing gum** is it's the most un-allowed thing you can do in school.

Or rather can't do in school. Even Jack Beechwhistle wouldn't eat chewing gum inside actual school, which is why he'd waited till he got just outside the school gates before he had started chewing.

When he came up to us, I forgot I was meant to be ignoring him. I told him that if I ever saw him eating chewing gum even a millimetre inside the school gates, I would tell Mrs Peters, the dinner ladies AND Mr Copford that he had brought chewing gum into school.

Jack said he didn't care, because he'd swallow it before they caught him. Then he told us it wasn't ordinary chewing gum either. It was NEW SPORTS CHEWING GUM!

When I asked Gabby if new sports chewing gum would help his legs run faster, she said she didn't know, which meant it might, which made me want to scream! I mean, not only did Jack Beechwhistle have new trainers to make him go faster and a new headband to make him go faster and new wristbands to make him go faster, now he had new sports chewing gum to help him go faster, too!!!!

It was so unfair!

When Gabby asked Jack to show her the packet, he said he wouldn't, because new sports chewing gum was for proper athletes only, not losers.

I said I'd rather be a loser than a pooser, which made Gabby really laugh.

And Harry Bayliss.

It even made Jack stop chewing.

Then, before he had time to think of a new name to call me back, Mum turned up to collect me, so he couldn't call me anything! Or even do a Usain Bolt point at me!! All he could do was frown!

Because my mum was there!

He did open his mouth really wide
so I could see all of his chewed-up
chewing gum, though.

Honestly, that boy is so childish.

On our way home with Mum, Gabby told me that losing wasn't in her vocabulary. And it shouldn't be in mine either. She said that if we used my Go for Gold Training and Eating Plan to train our very hardest at the weekend, then she was absolutely sure we would be able to win our different Sports Day races without the help of new trainers, new headbands, new wristbands or anything!

So that's what we decided to do. We decided we would help each other train and train and train ALL

weekend. I would help her to get brilliant at sprinting and she would help me to get brilliant at egg and spooning.

Provided I could get some more eggs.

The **trouble with getting some more eggs** is if you've already broken twelve in training, your mum might not want to buy you any more for a while.

Even if you keep telling her that you really fancy an omelette.

I told my mum that I fancied an omelette about seven times on the way home from school. She kept pretending not to hear me. Or even see me!

Gabby said that she might be able to get me some eggs from her house, but that if she asked for boiled eggs for tea on a Friday it might look a bit suspicious. (Gabby always has fish and chips for tea on Fridays and her mum and dad know that fish and chips is her favourite.)

Then she told me that if she asked for boiled eggs for breakfast on Saturday morning instead of Friday evening then it wouldn't look suspicious at all, unless she asked for too many.

I said that if boiled eggs are impossible to break then I would only need one or two. So that's what we decided to do. On Saturday morning we would meet up again. Gabby would bring the eggs and I would bring the spoon and at nine o'clock on Saturday morning our Go for Gold Olympic training would really begin!

And not in my back garden either! On the pavement outside my house!!!!!

# CHAPTER 10

When I woke up on Saturday morning, I got dressed really quickly, put my trainers on really quickly, ate my Weetabix really quickly, washed my face really quickly, cleaned my teeth really quickly and then waited outside by my front hedge hoping that Gabby would arrive really quickly.

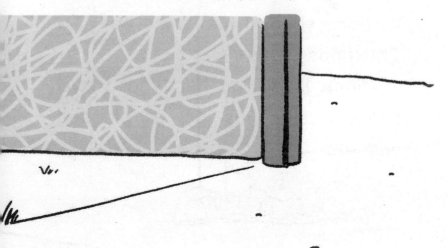

When she did, not only did she have two hard-boiled eggs for me to train with, she had brought a sports whistle for us to blow, too! It was exactly the same as Mr Copford's whistle, except it was made of yellow plastic, it didn't have a string and, instead of coming from a sports shop, it had come out of a Christmas cracker.

When I showed her what I had brought, she was just as pleased with me!

I'd brought the spoons.
I'd brought a pad to write our PBs on.

Plus I'd even remembered to bring a piece of chalk!

Chalk is the most important thing you can get in athletics because without chalk you can't see where a race starts and where it finishes.

After we'd drawn a big white start line on the pavement outside my house, Gabby told me that if we did sixty whopping strides up the road we could work out where the finish line should go.

So that's what we did. We did sixty whopping strides all the way up the pavement, counting as we went, past Dylan's house, and almost nearly right up to the top of the road!

Once our running track was absolutely ready, we started to jump up and down and shake our legs like proper athletes do. Then I got our Go for Gold Exercise and Training Plan out of my pocket.

The **trouble with a hundred sit-ups** is they really hurt your tummy.

So we only did three of those.

The **trouble with a hundred press-ups** is they really make your arms ache, even if you stick your bottom right up into the air. So we only did one of those.

The **trouble with a hundred running-on-the-spots** is we had already done a load of running-on-the-spots in rehearsals on Monday.

So we only did about seven of those.

The **trouble with doing all the other things on our exercise plan** was everything we tried left us more and more out of puff.

Plus I was busting to have a go with a hard-boiled egg.

So we decided to go straight to the racing bit instead.

When I put my first hard-boiled egg on my spoon, I was so excited I could have burst!

Gabby said that once I was standing with my feet behind the start line, she would run up to the finish line, blow the whistle and then start counting straight away. Trouble is, then she did a really loud practise whistle when I wasn't ready, which made me drop my first-ever hard-boiled egg on the pavement.

The **trouble with dropping your first-ever hard-boiled egg on the pavement** is you hardly dare open your eyes in case it's smashed all over the pavement.

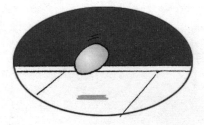

But it hadn't! Even though the shell was crunched a little bit, no runny stuff had come out at all! Which meant I could just put it straight back onto my spoon!

These are the PBs I did when I started my proper sixty-metre egg and spoon training with Gabby:

PB 1: (whitey-brown egg) 46 counts (7 drops)
PB 2: (whitey-brown egg) 45 and a bit counts (6 drops)
PB 3: (whitey-brown egg) 44 counts (5 drops)
PB 4: (whitey-brown egg) 43 and a bit counts (5 drops)
PB 5: (whitey-brown egg) 41 counts (2 drops)

PB 6: (whitey-brown egg) 40 and two smidgy bits counts (2 drops)

PB 7: (whitey-brown egg) 40 and a weensy smidge counts (2 drops)

PB 8: (whitey-brown egg) 39 and three quarter counts (nearly only 2 drops)

PB 9: (browny-white egg) 39 and a half counts (2 drops)

PB 10: (browny-white egg) 38 counts (1 drop)

PB 11: (browny-white egg) 37 and a half counts (1 drop)

PB 12: (browny-white egg) 37 and a quarter counts (1 drop)

PB 13: (browny-white egg) 36 counts (1 drop)

And these are the sprinting PBs that Gabby did when it was my turn to have a blow of the whistle:

PB 1: 16 counts
PB 2: 15 and three bits counts
PB 3: 15 and a half counts
PB 4: 15 and a tidgy bit counts
PB 5: 14 and three quarter counts
PB 6: 14 and a weensy tidge counts
PB 7: 14 counts
PB 8: 13 and a widdly biddly bit counts
PB 9: Nearly thirteen counts

After we'd been
training for about
an hour, Gabby said
that I was
definitely
getting better at
running with an egg
and a spoon, and

that once I had
learned to go the
whole sixty metres
without
my egg
dropping
off at all, I would
totally be able to beat

Lottie and Dottie. When I did my fourteenth PB, I actually DID manage to run the whole sixty metres without my egg falling off my spoon at all!

Even better, Dylan saw me do it! Dylan is a boy who lives in my street. He's two years older than me, plus he plays guitar, which means he's really cool.

133

Dylan said he had heard us blowing our whistle and had come out to see what we were doing. When he found out that we were going for gold, he was really impressed. When he found out that we had a Go for Gold Exercise and Training Plan plus a Go for Gold Eating Plan, as well as a whistle, things got even better, because then he offered to be our sports psychologist! For nothing!

Dylan said that sports psychologists can take athletes to a whole new level, and that if we wanted, he would give us a demonstration of how to do it.

Gabby said that she definitely wanted to move to a whole new level.

And I did too.

So Dylan went back into his house to get his skateboard.

# CHAPTER 11

The **trouble with skateboards** is they are even harder to get used to than eggs and spoons.

Dylan said that when he first got on his skateboard, he used to fall off all the time, but once he'd taught himself sports psychology, he had totally worked out how to stay on. Then he said that if we let him teach us, Gabby would totally run faster than she'd ever run before and my eggs would totally stay on my spoon.

Which sounded really simple.

But then it got a bit more complicated.

The **trouble with sports psychology** is Gabby and me couldn't really understand how it worked at all, even after Dylan had explained it.

According to Dylan, there are two things that athletes have to learn to do if they want to go to the next level.

The first thing they have to do is focus.

The second thing they have to do is clear their mind.

Trouble is, when I focused, I couldn't

clear my mind and when I cleared my
mind, I couldn't focus.

And neither could Gabby.

So Dylan showed us some
really good skateboard moves to

demonstrate how good going to the next level could be.

The **trouble with watching really good skateboard moves** is they make you want to do really good skateboard moves as well, even if you're not very good on a skateboard.

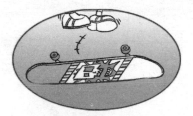

Dylan said that if we cleared our mind and focused at the same time, we would totally be able to be as good as him on a skateboard.

So we decided to have a try.

Well, Gabby did.

I was going to have the second try,
but when Gabby hit the lamppost, I
didn't really get the chance.

The **trouble with hitting a lamppost on a skateboard** is it really hurts, because skateboards go really fast.

The **trouble with hitting a lamppost on a skateboard with a whistle in your mouth** is it makes it a lot, lot worse. Especially if you nearly swallow the whistle.

As soon as me and Dylan had seen Gabby going out of control we tried to run and stop her, but everything happened so fast there wasn't very much that we could do.

Except help sit her up and pat her on the back really hard.

When the whistle came out of Gabby's mouth, Dylan and me were really relieved, because we thought she might have actually swallowed it. But I think Gabby was the one who was relieved the most.

Once she had stopped choking, she told us that she felt OK, but that she would like to sit on the pavement for a little while longer just to get her breath back. So we sat down on the pavement with her. Well, I did. Dylan had to go and get his skateboard from the middle of the road.

When he came back, he said that Gabby had probably focused on the lamppost by mistake instead of her skateboard skills, and that next time she should try it without the whistle.

But Gabby said she was retiring from skateboarding and that from now on she would just be doing sixty-metre sprinting instead.

Except she wouldn't. Because the next thing she tried to do was stand up.

The **trouble with trying to stand up** is sometimes it can be really difficult.

Especially if you've crashed into a lamppost and broken your ankle!

# CHAPTER 12

The **trouble with breaking your ankle** is it really, really hurts. Even if you haven't broken your ankle.

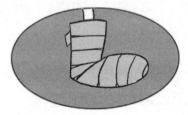

I was sooooo relieved when Gabby rang me from the hospital to tell me her ankle wasn't actually broken. She said a doctor had done loads of tests on it and that because she could still wiggle her foot, it meant it wasn't broken, but really badly sprained instead.

When I told her that her voice sounded really badly sprained too, she said that was because she had

nearly swallowed a whistle. Plus she had some really bad news to tell me.

When I asked her what her news was she said it was so bad that it was probably going to sprain my ears when I heard it.

And she was right. The next bit of news was so terrible, it sprained my ears, my lips, my teeth and my eyebrows. In fact, it nearly made me drop the phone.

You've guessed it, haven't you? Gabby had sprained her ankle so badly that the doctor had told her SHE WOULDN'T BE ABLE TO RUN ON SPORTS DAY!

Which meant now I would have to go for gold on my own, without anyone to train with or anyone to count my PBs or whistle at me or help me at all!

Gabby said that once her dad had driven her back from the hospital she still might be able to get me some more eggs, but because she was going to be on crutches for a while, I might have to call round to her house to get them.

**That's the trouble with crutches.** They're not as easy to use as normal feet.

When I asked Gabby if she was going to be able to go to school on Monday, she said she didn't think so. When I asked her if she would be able to go to school on Sports Day, she said she didn't know that either.

In fact, she didn't even know if she would ever be able to walk again!

Or run.

Or skip.

Or dance.

Or hop.

Or even smile.

Then the credit ran out on her dad's phone. Which was a good job really, because she was actually making me quite miserable.

The **trouble with being quite miserable** is it's better if you can be really miserable instead. That way your mum will feel sorry for you quicker.

When my mum realized that I was really miserable, she sat down beside me on the sofa and put her arm round me. She even offered to buy me some more eggs!

When I told her that Gabby and me had been training really, really hard

together and that she had crashed
into a lamppost and wouldn't even be
able to run in her race on Wednesday
and that she might not even be able

to come to school and see me run in mine, Mum said that in that case there was only one thing I could do.

Stay positive. (Which was one thing.)

Carry on with my egg and spoon training. (Which was two things!)

Stay away from lampposts. (Which was three things!!!)

Try my very hardest to win my race on Sports Day. (Which was four things!!!!)

And if I did win my race on Sports Day, I should dedicate my win to Gabby. (Which was five things!!!!!)

When I asked my mum what

dedicate meant, she said it meant telling Gabby that I would never have been able to win my race without all the help she had given me.

Which was true!

Mum said that if I won my race and dedicated my win to Gabby it would mean that both Gabby AND me were winners, even though Gabby had been unable to do a race of her own.

Which was even better!

So that's what we decided to do. I would try as hard as I could to win my race for me and for Gabby. And my mum would try as hard as she could to help me.

Which was even better than even better!

Because if my mum was going to try and help me win as much as she could, at last I had a chance to show her my Go for Gold Eating Plan.

# CHAPTER 13

The **trouble with Go for Gold Eating Plans** is mums don't really understand them.

When I told her that all the top athletes eat cheese strings, dry-roasted peanuts and Mars bars before a race she said that she wasn't sure that was actually true.

When she asked me if I might want to add some other healthy things to my plan, like potatoes and pasta and chicken and fish and fresh vegetables, I said they sounded a bit boring and anyway it was my eating plan and I knew what foods would make me go faster better than anyone.

But she wasn't sure that was actually true either.

So she told me to re-write my plan.

Luckily I didn't have to, because just as I was going to get my pencil case, Gabby rang me again from her house phone, which meant she was home from hospital!

As soon as I picked up the phone, Gabby told me all about her new

crutches. She said they felt totally weird, especially under her armpits, plus when she walked they made a click-click-clicking sound, and they smelled funny, and they made her hands sore, but it was totally worth it, because once she got going she could do massive hops and swing her feet just like Tarzan!

When I told her that I would be dedicating my win to her if I won on Sports Day, she forgot all about her crutches and did a really big squeal. In fact, her squeal was so squeally that it really did sound like she had swallowed that whistle!

Once she'd stopped squealing, she said that having a race dedicated to her would be the proudest moment in her athletics career.

Gabby said she was sure that if I carried on training really hard I would be able to win my race for both of us!

I told her that I was absolutely sure I would too.

Trouble is, I wasn't.

The **trouble with running a race for two people** is that when you sit down and really think about things, it begins to feel twice as hard.

Because two people is twice as many people as one person. Which means if you don't actually manage to win your race, it will probably feel twice as bad.

Because you'll be twice as disappointed if you lose.

When Mum and me got back from shopping on Saturday afternoon, I went straight out into my back garden with a new hard-boiled egg. But I still found it hard to keep it on my spoon. I was definitely getting quicker, but every time my egg got fidgety, my fingers sort of panicked a bit and jiggled it off the spoon.

Mum said I should trust to the force, but I told her only Jedi Knights did that.

So she told me to trust to some carrot sticks instead.

The **trouble with carrot sticks** is they are nowhere near as good for you as Mars bars, cheese strings and dry-roasted peanuts.

But Mum said the very least I could do was give them a try.

So I did.

But she was still definitely wrong.

It was the same when I trusted to a glass of milk instead of lemonade.

When I did my training again on Sunday, I felt really tired all day, because I had spent most of Saturday night worrying about running for two.

Mum said if I was so worried about running for Gabby as well as me, then I should ring Gabby up and tell her that I had changed my mind and would be running just for myself instead.

But I said I couldn't do that, because Gabby was my best friend and she had a really bad sports injury and I didn't want to let her down.

When I woke up on Monday morning, I felt absolutely exhausted, because just before I had gone to bed on Sunday night, Gabby had rung me up to tell me that I was running for her teddy too.

Which meant instead of running

for two people, now I was running for three!!!

By the time I got to school, I could barely keep my eyes open.

# CHAPTER 14

The **trouble with not keeping your eyes open** is it can really hurt. Especially if you fall forward in assembly and bonk your nose on Jasmine Smart.

I didn't actually realize I'd fallen asleep in assembly. Everyone else did. Trouble is, nobody woke me.

The **trouble with nobody waking you** is when you do wake up you can't be sure how much of assembly you've missed.

It must have been quite a lot, because after we'd sung a song to Jesus, the only thing Mr Copford had left to tell us was his Thought for Sports Day Week.

The **trouble with Thoughts for Sports Day Week** is they can be even more confusing than Thoughts for a Normal Week!

I actually thought I was dreaming when Mr Copford gave us his Thought for Sports Day Week, because do you know what it was?

I couldn't believe it.

Neither could Sanjay Lapore or Barry Morely or Fiona Tucker or anyone in my class.

Mr Copford's Thought for Sports Day Week was:

**IT'S NOT THE WINNING. IT'S THE TAKING PART!**

When we got back to our classroom after assembly, everyone was totally confused. Even once Mrs Peters had explained exactly what Mr Copford meant, we were still confused. I mean, just last Monday, Mr Copford had told us all to go for gold. Now he was telling us that winning isn't important and that just trying your best is what counts.

How confusing is that!?

Jack Beechwhistle said there was no way he wasn't going for gold, especially with all the new things he had to help him win.

Paula Potts said she didn't even see the point of throwing a foam javelin if you weren't going to win.

Colin Kettle said losing was for losers.

Bernadette Laine said silver medals were for wimps.

Stephanie

Brakespeare said bronzes were for wusses.

And Lottie and Dottie Taylor said there was absolutely no way that they would be going for anything other than gold on Sports Day, especially after all the egg time they had put in over the weekend.

That was the moment I realized
Lottie and Dottie Taylor had been
doing Olympic training too!

# CHAPTER 15

When I asked Lottie and Dottie what kind of egg time they had been putting in over the weekend, I nearly fainted.

They said their dad had come up with a training plan called Eggstreme Coaching.

That's the **trouble with dads who are gym instructors**. They are dads who are gym instructors.

When Lottie and Dottie told me what Eggstreme Coaching meant, I was so shocked I had to go and sit down on the quiet bench. Because Lottie and Dottie had spent their entire identical weekend with an egg and spoon in their hand! They had eaten their breakfast with an egg  and spoon in their hand, they had put their dishes in the dishwasher with an egg and spoon in

their hand, they had cleaned their teeth with an egg and spoon in their hand, they had

washed their dad's car with an egg and spoon in their hand, they had done their homework with

an egg and spoon in their hand, they had ridden their bikes with an egg and

spoon in their hand, they had even

gone to the loo with an egg and
spoon in their hand.

Without dropping even one of
their eggs once! I mean, how scary
is that!

As soon as I found out that
Lottie and Dottie had been doing
Eggstreme Coaching I absolutely
knew that I had no chance of

winning a Sports Day race for me and Gabby or her teddy.

Mum said if I was so worried about racing for three against Lottie and Dottie then I should pick up the phone and explain things to Gabby right away.

So I tried.

But the **trouble with calling Gabby** is the moment she heard my voice she did a big squeal.

She said she was so excited about having a race dedicated to her that she had told absolutely everyone she knew.

She had told her mum.

And her dad.

And her nana.

And her grandpa.

And her aunt.

And her uncle.

She'd told the postman.

She'd told the doctor who had re-pinned her bandage that morning.

She had even told the car park man at the hospital.

When I told her about Mr Copford's Thought for Sports Day Week, she nearly choked. She said that winning a race was FAR more exciting than coming second or third or fourth or fifth or definitely last in a race. Especially if the race that you have won has been DEDICATED TO YOU!

So I didn't tell her about Lottie and Dottie after that.

I just decided that I needed to get faster. And I needed to get faster FAST!

# CHAPTER 16

The **trouble with getting faster FAST**
is there was only one way I could
think of doing it.

And it was the most horrible,
disgusting, embarrassing way in the
world!

I had to get up on Tuesday morning.

I had to get dressed for school.

I had to go into school.

I had to walk into the playground . . .

I had to find Jack Beechwhistle . . .

. . . and ask him to give me some of his new sports chewing gum.

The **trouble with asking Jack Beechwhistle for ANYTHING** is I don't like Jack Beechwhistle.

And he doesn't like me.

Plus I didn't have any money to pay him.

Which is why he said, "No way."

The **trouble with Jack Beechwhistle saying no way** is I didn't have any ways left.

So I was forced to say please.

But he still said no way.

So I was forced to say please with sugar on top.

But he still said no way.

So I was forced to say please with sugar and a cherry on top.

But he still said no way.

So I had to say I would do anything.

The **trouble with saying I would do anything** is it made him do one of his horrible smiles.

"I'll give you ONE piece of my new sports chewing gum," he said, "IF . . ."

"If what?" I said.

"IF . . ." he said.

"If what?" I said.

"IF," he said, "you say . . . I'M THE BEST!"

The **trouble with saying Jack Beechwhistle is the best** is he's not the best, he's the worst.

But I really wanted to win my race for Gabby.

So I said it.

Even though I didn't mean it.

The **trouble with saying it even though you don't mean it** is it made him think of something else for me to do.

"I'll give you TWO pieces of my new sports chewing gum," he said, "IF . . ."

"If what?" I said.

"IF . . ." he said.

"If what?" I said.

"IF," he said, "you say . . . I'M THE KING!"

The **trouble with saying Jack Beechwhistle is the king** is he's not the king. He's a King Kong Monkey Face.

But I really, really wanted to win my race for Gabby.

And her teddy.

So I said it.

Even though I really, really didn't mean it.

The **trouble with saying it even though you really, really don't mean it** is it made him think of the worst possible thing in the whole world that he could make me do . . . !

"I'll give you **A WHOLE PACKET** of my new sports chewing gum," he said, "IF . . ."

"If what?" I said.

"IF . . ." he said.

"If what?" I said.

"IF," he said, "**YOU KISS MY TRAINERS!**"

The **trouble with kissing Jack Beechwhistle's trainers** is I'd rather kiss a baboon on the bottom.

When I told him he wasn't wearing trainers, he said he had them in his school bag and I could kiss them after school. Not only that, he said I could kiss them in front of my mum!

The **trouble with kissing Jack Beechwhistle's trainers in front of my mum** is there is absolutely NO WAY I would kiss Jack Beechwhistle's trainers in front of my mum!

Unless I was desperate to win a race for Gabby.

When I asked him if his trainers would still be in his bag, or on his feet, he said he would keep them in his bag.

So I asked him how fast a whole packet of new sports chewing gum would make me run.

Jack said that his new sports chewing gum was absolutely packed with super turbo running powers. In fact, once, after he'd eaten about four packets, he started running and almost broke the sound barrier.

The **trouble with breaking the sound barrier doing an egg and spoon race** is teachers would get suspicious.

So he said if I ate just one whole packet before my race, I would still definitely run easily fast enough to beat Lottie and Dottie. As long as I could keep my egg on its spoon as well.

So I asked him how many pieces were in a packet.

When he said there were eight pieces, I asked him if I could have my first two pieces now, but he said that there was no way he would risk being seen by a teacher with chewing gum in school. He would only give them to me when we were out of school.

So I asked him how long a packet's worth of running power would last me.

Jack said if I ate the whole packet of new sports chewing gum for my breakfast and chewed every last bit of flavour and goodness out on the way to school, my turbo powers would last at least until lunch time.

So I said I would: I said I would kiss his trainers.

Even though I REALLY, REALLY, REALLY didn't want to, I said I actually actually would!

BECAUSE I JUST HAD TO WIN MY EGG AND SPOON RACE FOR GABBY!

# CHAPTER 17

When I got up this morning, all I could think about was winning my race for Gabby.

The new sports chewing gum Jack

had given me was hidden under my pillow. It was quite a funny-looking packet. In fact, it didn't have any writing on it at all. Jack said his dad had got a whole box straight from the chewing gum factory before the writing had even been printed on it! Which meant it was the freshest type of chewing gum you could get.

All I had to do now was chew it.

The **trouble with eating chewing gum for breakfast** is it's really difficult.

Especially if you've got to eat two Weetabixes first.

The **trouble with Weetabixes** is they are quite mushy in your mouth, especially if you have them with lots of milk.

I wasn't sure what would happen if I mixed the mush of my Weetabixes up with the chew of my chewing gums, so I decided to do my chews after I got dressed.

Because it was Sports Day, we

didn't have to wear our uniforms to school this morning. We were allowed to wear our PE kit instead! So once I'd done up my trainers and put my Tagliatelle PE top on, I locked the bathroom door, cleaned my teeth as quickly as I could and then put all eight pieces into my mouth at once.

The **trouble with putting eight pieces of chewing gum into your mouth all at once** is it makes it really hard to chew.

And it makes your eyes water.

At first it felt like I was chewing lolly sticks, but after a while the chewing gum pieces started to go softer.

By the time I left for school with Mum, I'd got my chewing gum really chewy. Plus I could feel some of the chewing gum super turbo powers building up in my dribble and then moving down into my legs.

When we got to the school gates, things got even more exciting, because all of the children in my year had their PE kits on and looked like they were definitely going for gold. Plus there was a massive queue of parents outside the school gates waiting to come in and watch!

When my mum went to queue up with all the parents, I hid behind the oak tree outside our school gates and chewed and chewed and chewed as much of the turbo power out of my chewing gum as I could.

Trouble is, then the school bell rang, so I had to stop, because you're not allowed chewing gum in school.

The **trouble with having to stop** is I was sure there was some super turbo power still left inside my gum, so I stayed behind the tree and kept on chewing.

When Jack Beechwhistle tapped me on my shoulder, I nearly jumped out of my skin because I thought it was a teacher. But when I saw his

headband and wristbands and new trainers I realized it wasn't.

Jack said that if I couldn't taste very much of my chewing gum any more then I had probably got all of the turbo powers out. Then he said if I didn't spit my chewing gum out really fast and run into school I would get into trouble.

So I did. I spat my chewing gum out and ran into school.

On the way into class, Jack asked me if my legs had begun to feel any faster after chewing his new sports chewing gum. When I said I could definitely feel turbo powers in my legs, he said that by the time Sports Day started, I would probably be getting turbo feelings all the way through my body.

And he was right!

# CHAPTER 18

When I ran out onto the field with my class, I felt like I could win any race in the world!

When I sat down beside the running track, I especially made sure that my legs stayed uncrossed, so that the super turbo powers could keep flowing.

There were rows and rows of parents sitting on the other side of the running track.

At first I thought my mum might have gone home, but then I saw her sitting right at the very top by the finish line.

As soon as I saw her, I gave her a big wave. As soon as she saw me back, she gave me a wave and a big thumbs-up, too!

At first, when I saw her do her big thumbs-up, I thought she was wishing me good luck. But then when she moved to one side, I realized what she was really saying.

Gabby had come to watch me run my race, too!

On her crutches!

When I saw Gabby standing beside Mum on her crutches, my chewing gum turbo powers went right down into my toes and right up into my hair. I couldn't believe that my best friend would come all the way into school just to watch me run my Sports Day race.

On her actual crutches!

If I was determined to win my race for Gabby before, I was even more determined now!

When Mrs Peters started giving eggs and spoons to everyone who was going to be in my race, I decided to start warming up straight away.

I stood up and wiggled my legs.

I touched my toes.

I put my egg on my spoon.

I emptied my mind. I totally focused . . . Trouble is, then I saw Lottie and Dottie warming up, too.

The **trouble with seeing Lottie and Dottie warming up** is it made my eyeballs nearly fall out.

Because do you know what Lottie and Dottie were doing for their warm-up? They were doing keepy-uppies with eggs and spoons!!! They were throwing and catching, spinning and catching, juggling and catching, even doing star jumps and catching! Lottie and Dottie could do things with eggs and spoons that even a chicken couldn't do!

As soon as I saw Lottie and Dottie doing keepy-uppies, I started to get a bit nervous.

As soon as I started to get a bit nervous, I started to get a bit worried.

As soon as I started to get a bit worried, I started to get funny feelings in my tummy.

As soon as I got funny feelings in my tummy, I started to get funny feelings in my head.

What if my new sports chewing gum super turbo powers weren't super turbo enough?

What if they ran out halfway through the race?

What if my laces came undone again?

What if my egg wouldn't stay on my spoon?

"MRS PETERS!" I shouted. "Please may I go to the loo?!"

# CHAPTER 19

The **trouble with going to the loo during lessons** is usually you can't go and get your school bag to take to the loo with you.

But this morning no one could stop me, because my whole classroom was empty because everyone was out on the field. Including Mrs Peters!

Once I had sat down on the loo with my school bag on my lap, I started to feel much better. By the time I had done what I needed to do, put my school bag back on its hook and run back onto the field, I was absolutely sure I could still win my race. Even if Lottie and Dottie could do eggy keepy-uppies!

When I got back and sat down on the field, I didn't have any idea at all which house was winning. According to Melanie Simpson, Liberty Pearce (Linguine) had won the sack race, someone from class 4B (no idea) had won the long-distance for girls, David Alexander (Fettuccine) had won the long-distance for boys, Nishta Baghwat (Tagliatelle!) had come first in the obstacle race, and a boy from 4C (doesn't matter) had been disqualified in the foam javelin.

Bernadette Laine reckoned Fettuccine might be in the lead to win the house cup and Daniel McNicholl

thought it might be Penne, but I
wasn't really listening.

All I could think about was
winning my race for Gabby. Even

when Tagliatelle came first, second and third in the multi-skills, all I could think about was winning my race for Gabby.

When the time came for me to actually run my race, I think I'd gone into a rather strange zone. In fact, Mrs Peters had to tap me on my head with a spoon to get me to walk to the start line.

When I saw Lottie and Dottie lining up too, my heart started to beat really fast.

When I put my egg on my spoon and held it out in front of me, my legs started to rev really fast too.

"ON YOUR MARKS . . ." said Mrs Peters.

"GET SET . . ." said Mrs Peters.

As soon as Mrs Peters said, "GO!" everyone in my whole year stood up and started to scream and shout the names of their houses!

"PENNE! PENNE!"

"TAGLIATELLE! TAGLIATELLE!"

They probably shouted Fettuccine and Linguine too, but to be honest, I didn't hear anything after that, because I was too busy running.

And running and running and running!

The **trouble with running and running and running** is it makes your heart and your eyeballs really shake.

When I looked to my left, I could see Lottie and Dottie right alongside me!

When I looked to my right, I couldn't see anyone at all!

MY TURBO POWERS WERE WORKING! MY TURBO POWERS WERE WORKING!

When I looked in front of me, my egg was still on my spoon!

MY EGG WAS STAYING ON! MY EGG WAS STAYING ON!

*Drop your eggs! Drop your eggs!* I thought, hoping that Lottie and Dottie would have an accident with their spoons.

But when I looked to my left, I saw they were still level.

*COME UNDONE, COME UNDONE!* I thought, hoping that Lottie and Dottie would have an accident with their laces.

But when I looked to my left, I saw that we were level STILL!

I WAS WINNING! I WAS WINNING!
Or at least I WAS LEVEL! I WAS LEVEL!
*WIN IT FOR GABBY! WIN IT FOR
GABBY!* I thought, using all of my
new sports chewing gum super turbo
powers to keep my trainers going.

"DON'T LOOK LEFT, JUST LOOK FORWARD. DON'T LOOK LEFT, JUST LOOK FORWARD," I gasped as I saw the finish line approaching!

"STAY ON, EGG! STAY ON, EGG!" I panted, stretching my egg and spoon out as far as I could reach.

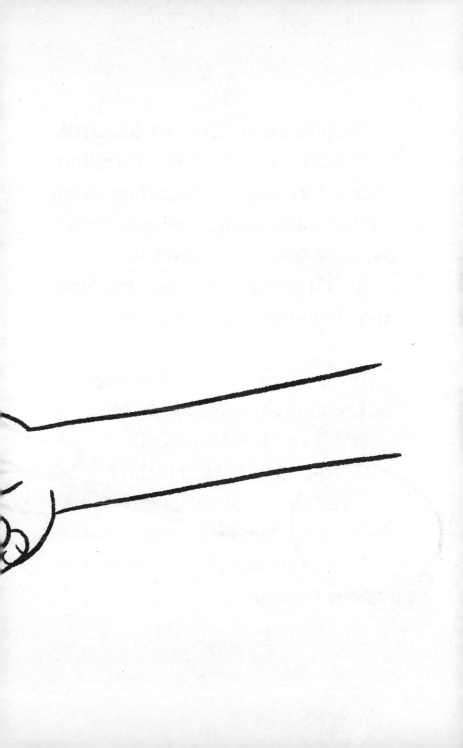

"YOU CAN DO IT, LUCKY EGG! YOU CAN DO IT, LUCKY EGG!" I gasped, shutting my eyes tight and then diving for the finish line with my spoon stuck out as far as I could stretch!

As I crossed the line, my ears burst with the sound of children and parents cheering.

The instant I opened my eyes, I looked straight across to Gabby.

HAD I WON? HAD I WON?

Or HAD I LOST? HAD I LOST?

I was so out of puff, I didn't even notice Mrs Palmer putting a sticker on my PE top. But when I looked at it, I nearly fainted!

Because the number on the sticker wasn't a two or a three, it was a ONE!

No wonder Gabby was cheering. No wonder Gabby was waving her crutches!

I HAD WON! I HAD WON! I HAD WON THE RACE FOR GABBY!!!!

As soon as I realized I had won, I ran straight over to Gabby, her teddy and Mum and gave them all a big hug!

"I WON! I WON!" I shouted.

"YOU ALL WON! YOU ALL WON!" said Gabby.

"IT WAS A THREE-WAY TIE! IT WAS A THREE-WAY TIE!" said Mum. "IT WAS A THREE-WAY TIE FOR FIRST PLACE!"

The **trouble with a three-way tie for first place** is I wasn't exactly sure what that meant.

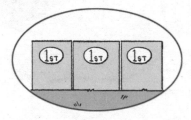

But when I looked round at Lottie and Dottie, I worked it out straight away. Because not only was I wearing a winner sticker on my PE top, Lottie and Dottie were both wearing one too! Which meant we had ALL come first at exactly the same time!

When I realized that I had come joint-joint first, I was SO excited.

Because now I could dedicate my joint-joint win to Gabby!

And her teddy!

I couldn't believe I'd done it! After all the training and chewing I'd done, it was so amazing!

It was so brilliant! It was so fab! If only Lottie and Dottie hadn't had a gym instructor dad.

# CHAPTER 20

The **trouble with gym instructor dads** is they only want their own children to win races.

When Mrs Palmer said that we had all run such a good race and that there really was no way of separating us, Lottie and Dottie's dad said that there most certainly was. He said that when a race ends in a photo finish, all you need to separate the winners from the losers is a photo.

Mrs Palmer said that he might be right, but she didn't have a photo.

Trouble is, Lottie and Dottie's dad did.

The **trouble with camera phones** is they have cameras on them. Which means they can take pictures of things like people smiling, or people dancing, or three people crossing a finish line at the same time.

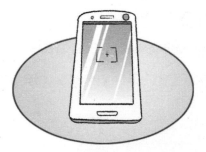

When Lottie and Dottie's dad took his camera phone out of his pocket, my mum went doolally.

She said she could not believe that a parent would be so competitive and so pushy and so stupid as to take a photo of three children crossing a finish line at the same time.

But Lottie and Dottie's dad wouldn't listen. He said his daughters had never lost a race of any kind in their life and they weren't about to start sharing their victories now.

When my mum started hitting

him on the head with Gabby's teddy,
it got really embarrassing. Because
instead of all the children in my year
shouting, "Penne!" or "Tagliatelle!"
they started shouting, "FIGHT! FIGHT!
FIGHT!" instead.

Which meant Mr Copford got
involved too.

The **trouble with Mr Copford getting involved** is once he'd made my mum give him Gabby's teddy, he asked to see the photo on Lottie and Dottie's dad's phone.

The **trouble with the photo on Lottie and Dottie's dad's phone** is it definitely proved that we had all crossed the line at identically the same time.

Trouble is, when you looked at it really closely you could see that my egg and spoon was upside down.

The **trouble with eggs and spoons being upside down** is it looks like you've glued your egg to your spoon.

But I hadn't! I honestly, honestly hadn't.

I even took my egg off my spoon to prove it!

Trouble is, then Mr Copford asked to have a closer look.

The **trouble with asking to have a closer** look is I didn't really want anyone to hold my lucky egg except me.

But Mr Copford insisted.

Which is why I got sent to his office straight away.

# CHAPTER 21

The **trouble with going to the loo during Sports Day and then rolling a new lucky egg out of the chewing gum that you've spat into your school bag** is it's not really allowed.

It looks really good. In fact, after I had rolled all eight pieces worth of chewed-up chewing gum in the palms of my hands really carefully,

it ended up looking exactly the same colour and exactly the same shape as the ordinary egg Mrs Peters had given me.

Only it was better. Because ordinary eggs don't stick to spoons.

Which is why I put the ordinary egg back into my bag.

Mr Copford said he'd heard of people trying to glue their eggs to a spoon before, but he'd never heard of anyone making an entire egg out of gum.

At first I thought he was going to give me an extra house point for showing good craft skills, but

he didn't. He gave me a detention instead.

In fact, he gave me two detentions. One for cheating in Sports Day, and another for chewing chewing gum in school.

When I told him that I hadn't actually chewed chewing gum in school, I'd only rolled chewing gum in the palms of my hands in school, he gave me my third detention in a row.

When I got back to class, Mrs Peters told everyone that she was very disappointed by my lack of sportsmanship.

Which was really embarrassing.

Then she made me say sorry out loud to Lottie and Dottie. AND write a sorry letter to their dad.

Which was even more embarrassing.

Then I found out that Linguine had won the Sports Day house cup. Which was really annoying because Jack Beechwhistle is in Linguine.

When Jack asked me if I had told Mr Copford where I had got my chewing gum from, I said I hadn't.

But then I wished I had.

Because do you know what he said to me next? He said the chewing gum he'd given me wasn't even new sports chewing gum at all. It had been plain old ordinary normal chewing gum all along!

Which meant I'd kissed Jack Beechwhistle's trainers in front of my mum ALL FOR NOTHING!

And I'd told him he was the best!

AND I'd told him he was the king . . .

I'm so glad he only came fifth in his race!

When I met Mum after school, she was too embarrassed to wait by the school gate. She hid behind the oak tree instead.

On the way home, she told me that if I hadn't made an egg out of chewing gum, she would never have ended up hitting Lottie and Dottie's dad on the head with a teddy. She told me I had let myself down, I had let her down, I had let my teachers down, I had let Tagliatelle down. In fact, I'd let my whole school down.

Oh well, at least I hadn't let Gabby down.

When I went round to visit her after school, Gabby didn't seem let down at all. She was still really excited about almost nearly having a race dedicated to her. She let me have

a go on her crutches and showed
me how to do big hops and Tarzan
swings. She said she really couldn't
thank me enough. I even got a high-
five from her teddy.

When Gabby asked me if I wanted to stay for tea, I definitely should have said yes. Because when I got home and asked Mum what we were having to eat, all she gave me was an empty plate.

That's **the trouble with tea times when I've been naughty**.

No chef.

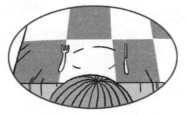

# DAISY'S
# TROUBLE INDEX

# The trouble with . . .

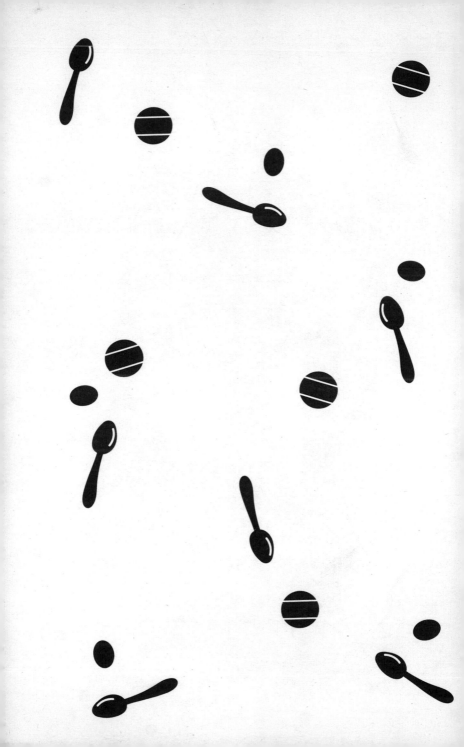